THE HUNTING GUN

Yasushi Inoue

THE HUNTING GUN

Translated from the Japanese
and with an Introduction by
Sadamichi Yokoö
and
Sanford Goldstein

PETER OWEN · LONDON

ISBN 0 7206 0754 X

PL
830
.N6
H8
1989

PETER OWEN PUBLISHERS
73 Kenway Road London SW5 0RE

First published in Great Britain 1989
© Charles E. Tuttle Company, Inc. 1961

Printed and bound in Great Britain by
Redwood Burn Limited Trowbridge Wiltshire

INTRODUCTION

In Yasushi Inoue's work as a whole, and in *The Hunting Gun* in particular, the theme of loneliness and isolation lends itself to the fusion of story and poem, a technique that has earned for Inoue a major role among the post-war writers of Japan.

The loneliness at the core of Inoue's creative activity is basically Oriental. It is not the loneliness of a person defeated in the struggle for life—one who has sadly discovered his inability to adapt—nor is it that of one too self-conscious to enter the arena of active life or too self-conscious to achieve any ties of affection. Oriental loneliness is related to the weariness of life and its negation. The heroes of Inoue's stories, most of them of the well-to-do middle class, are capable of worldly success, but temperamentally they feel that material success does not deserve their wholehearted devotion. Inoue suggests the importance of a warm personal relationship, but here, too, complete fulfillment is negated, for his characters feel that every man has a vital inner sphere (in *The Hunting Gun* it is called a small snake) from which other humans are barred. Consequently, Inoue's heroes find no social activities or personal relationships worthy of their deepest

5

passions. In some cases, like that of the hero of *The Hunting Gun*, they retire into the hard shell of their inner world to live a lonely, self-contained existence; in others, they plunge into the more arduous activities in order to stifle their feelings of futility and isolation, but they do so without success. The life struggle has lost its meaning; instead of affirmation there is negation. And yet humanity, overwhelmed by loneliness and isolation under Inoue's compassionate treatment, is not without recourse, for Inoue and his characters find some consolation in the world of nature.

Inoue's autobiographical *Story of an Arbor Vitae* (1953) underscores the loneliness of his own early years. Born May 6, 1907, at Asahikawa in Hokkaido, Yasushi was the first of Hayao Inoue's four children. The father, an army surgeon, was continually on the move, and finally Yasushi, on reaching school age, went to live with his grandmother in Izu, the mountainous peninsula southwest of Tokyo, its highest mountain Amagi, and Atami one of its flourishing hot-spring resorts.

In spite of the boy's affection for his grandmother, the isolation from his immediate family perhaps intensified his natural inclination for introspection and his consciousness of the need for affection. Later, in 1927, with the intention of following in his father's footsteps (in fact, in the tradition of the long line of doctors that ran in his family), Inoue entered the science course of a high school at Kanazawa. But it seems that judo was more appealing than study, and he did not attain the high grades essential for a student aspiring toward entrance into a medical school. After his graduation from high school in 1930, Inoue drifted into the literature course at Kyushu

University but again failed to attend classes. A great deal of his time was spent in distant Tokyo, where he read with intense interest whatever came his way, mostly Western literature in translation. Two years later he enrolled at Kyoto University to study aesthetics.

The study of aesthetics no doubt gave him materials with which to put his own creative talents to use. A number of his stories, in fact, are concerned with the problems of artists. Even before he began writing fiction, he had written essays on artists and their works. In addition, he was continuing to create his own lyric poems.

After his graduation from Kyoto University in 1936, Inoue became a reporter for the *Mainichi* at Osaka, one of the positions greatly desired by university graduates. His experience as a journalist (outside of a short term of duty in north China from September, 1937, to January, 1938, as a soldier in military transportation, he was to serve on the *Mainichi* until 1951) increased his awareness of the social forces in Japanese society. The unexplained death in 1949 of President Shimoyama of the National Railways Corporation, fictionalized in Inoue's *The Black Tide* (1950), is a case in point. In the novel Inoue probes the cause of that death in terms of its personal, economic, and political implications.

Inoue's stories may be divided into those concerned with social incidents, those with the artist-scholar, and those with history as their major background. *The Ice Bank* (1957), awarded the Academy Prize, focuses on the death of a mountain climber, an actual event which became the subject of a recent controversy about the strength of nylon rope. *Shikkoson* (1950) is about a lacquered vessel treasured for more than a thousand years

7

in a Nara storehouse. *Tiles of the Tempyo Era* (1957), awarded the Ministry of Education Prize for Literature, and *Tunhuang* (1959), awarded the Mainichi Press Prize, are historical novels about old China, the interest in which originated from Inoue's study of fine arts at Kyoto University. In spite of the fact that Inoue is one of Japan's most prolific writers, his thoroughness in collecting data (he climbed Mount Hodaka four times in gathering material for *The Ice Bank*) is proof that his stories, even the shortest, are not written perfunctorily. And whatever the work, it serves to illustrate his main theme of human loneliness.

In 1950, Inoue's two initial works, *The Hunting Gun* and *The Bull Fight,* both published in the preceding year, won for their author the coveted Akutagawa Prize, the most famous literary award in Japan. Mitsuo Nakamura, a leading critic of modern Japanese literature, believes that because Inoue began his career as a successful novelist rather late, at the age of forty-two, these two stories represent what the mature artist in Inoue has to express.

The narrator of *Ryoju,* or *The Hunting Gun,* is a poet with possibly the same touch of contempt for his poetry that Inoue himself felt about his own poems, collected in 1958 under the title of *The Northern Country.* The volume contains many poems which formed the germ for a number of successful stories. Writes Inoue: "I have been reading and writing poems ever since I was a middle-school boy, but the poems I have written in all those years are quite few. Those remaining in my notebooks are about fifty, including the fragmentary ones. . . . Again reading over my notebooks now, I find that these lines are not so much poetry as small boxes in which poetry is locked up

. . . these little lines in my notebooks are something from which, if some magic spell were cast upon them, real poems would emerge. Poetry in the strictest sense may be said to be that spell. . . . But I am a poet who has never succeeded in discovering the spell." What Inoue has done is to gather fictional materials around the core of a poem; poetry and story are dramatically integrated. One of these poems, only slightly changed from its later version in *The Northern Country,* appears at the beginning of *The Hunting Gun.*

The story deals with a love affair of upper middle-class people living at Ashiya, a wealthy suburb of the two great commercial cities of Osaka and Kobe. The postwar period of black marketeering and great social upheaval, with the traditionally rich and sophisticated in decline, finds the hero, Josuke Misugi, at one time a businessman in the upper echelons, purged by the Occupation.

The poet-narrator, coming upon the hero-hunter at the foot of Mount Amagi, is instantly attracted by the extremely lonesome figure. The sight lingers in the poet's mind. He himself has something in him that parallels the hunter's loneliness. The silent, cold, inviolate hunting gun seems to the poet to symbolize the hunter's lonely, self-contained existence. And in the poet's imagination the mountain path is transformed into a bleak white riverbed, a setting more suitable for a lonely hunter. Perhaps through some intuitive awareness of the poet's sensitivity and compassion, the hunter reveals to him what his environment and life and mind have been, what his white riverbed has been. In this way we are led into the lonely lives of three women and the main current of the story.

The love affair, like the gradual view of a riverbed seen through receding mist, is finally revealed in its entirety. Once more the lonely back of the hunter returns to the eyes of the poet. Once more he picks up the brief explanatory letter in which the hero notes that the hunting gun seemed indispensable to him no matter how successful his public and private affairs. The poet wonders what the revelations of the three women could have added then to the hunter's knowledge. Possibly nothing. For the hero must have known everything years ago. He must have known that the world is not one in which the desires of the heart are fulfilled; that as long as one lives, the individual heart holds its own secret; that the more one is faithful to oneself, the further one retires into his own inner world. Thus the seemingly irrelevant title of the story proves to be the symbol of its main motif. And still, as indispensable as the hunting gun was to the hero, the desire to love remains, the desire to communicate, to find one other human being who can understand. We are left with the dilemma of human loneliness.

The Hunting Gun started Inoue on his highly successful career and helped establish his present position in modern Japanese literature. The famous critic Kiyoshi Jinzai says that Inoue's work "at its deepest has something which may be called an old calmness . . . calm emotion flowing forever unchanging under social vicissitudes and turmoil." It is in this connection that the merging of poetry and story becomes apparent.

Earlier Japanese novelists had deliberately rejected the imaginative element in fiction. In the Tokugawa era (1603–1867), only literature that supported the codes of feudalism received approval from the ruling classes. Of course, popular novels about townsmen and their social customs and their amusing exploits were written and read, but these were regarded as inferior entertainment unworthy of the warrior class. The modern conception of serious literature began, it is generally agreed, with Shoyo Tsubouchi's novel *The Spirit of Modern Students* (1885), which illustrated its author's literary theory as presented in his essay of the same year, "The Quintessence of the Novel." Rejecting the conception of literature as propaganda, Tsubouchi asserted that the main object of literature was the realistic observation of human beings. This new approach resulted in the realistic presentation of characters, and novelists concentrated on living persons. The novelist's craft, consequently, came quite near that of landscape or portrait painting. In the same way that a portrait painter needed models, so the novelist required real persons to describe. In fact, the "models" of these Japanese stories often sued for libel.

Of course, this technique bordering on scientific accuracy could not prove of continual satisfaction to the artist. He had to express himself. But the theory of "realism" intruded here as well. The novelist stated his own experience, his own state of mind, so directly and so subjectively that the novel approached the autobiographical essay or the lyric poem, and the author presupposed himself admirable material for the reading public. The result was the "I" novel, the *watakushi-shosetsu,* which has been a major current in Japanese literature.

Obviously there have been other kinds of Japanese novels and novelists. The two famous novelists of modern Japan, Soseki Natsume (1867–1916) and Ogai Mori (1862–1922), are outside that main current with their knowledge, in Soseki's case, of psychology and, in Ogai's, of history. There is also a great body of "popular" literature which relies on the amusing situation. But novelists of "pure" literature—that is, of *watakushi-shosetsu*—retained for themselves the high seriousness of the poet and let the popular writers monopolize the amusing tale.

Recently the "I" novel has been subject to a good deal of critical abuse as being too barren, trivial, and subjective. But whatever its defects, its merit of high seriousness cannot be ignored. And this is especially laudable in Japan, where poetry has failed to reach a large audience. These modern "I" novels have been a source in satisfying the need for poetry in the Japanese reader.

The problem of the present-day novelist in Japan would seem to be to combine the high seriousness and lyrical quality of "pure" literature with the interesting story of "popular" consumption. It is this synthesis, found in *The Hunting Gun* and Inoue's work generally, which has been his major contribution to modern Japanese literature.

SADAMICHI YOKOÖ
Hiroshima University

SANFORD GOLDSTEIN
Nagasaki University

THE HUNTING GUN

To THE latest edition of *The Hunter's Companion,* a thin magazine put out by the Hunters Club of Japan, I contributed a poem called "Hunting Gun."

This may sound as though I were more or less interested in hunting, but the truth is that I was brought up by a mother who hated killing, and I have never even handled an air rifle. The explanation is quite simple: the fellow who edits *The Hunter's Companion* was my classmate in high school, and partly out of whim and partly, I suppose, as a polite expression of his regret over the way our friendship has declined, he asked me to send in a poem. Even though I'm getting on in years, I can't wash my hands of the coterie magazines, and I still scribble poems in my own way. At any rate, since *The Hunter's Companion* was quite foreign to my interests and since the editor had asked that the poem have something to do with hunting, at any other time I would have immediately refused to accept his offer. But just then I had been inspired by the relationship between a hunting gun and human loneliness, and I intended to write a poem about it.

One chilly night in late November I sat at my desk

until after midnight and wrote a prose-poem in my own fashion and rushed it off to the editor the next day.

Since the poem has something to do with the story I'm telling, I've decided to insert it here:

A large seaman's pipe in his mouth,
A setter running before him in grass,
The man strode up the early winter path of Mount
    Amagi,
And frost cracked under boot-sole.
The band with five and twenty bullets,
The leather coat, dark brown,
The double-barreled Churchill—
What made him cold, armed with white, bright steel,
To take the lives of creatures?

Attracted by the tall hunter's back,
I looked and looked.

Since that time,
At the stations of great cities,
Or at night in amusement quarters,
I sometimes dream:
I wish his life—
Slow, calm, cold.

Moments shift the hunting scene:
A bleak, white riverbed,
Not Mount Amagi's early winter cold.
And the glittering hunting gun,
Stamping its weight on the lonely body,
Lonely mind of a middle-aged man,

Radiates a queer, austere beauty,
Never shown when aimed at life.

When I received the issue my poem was in and ran over the pages, I found for the first time, stupidly enough, that in spite of its plausible title, the poem was entirely out of place in that magazine. It too obviously conflicted with "the morals of hunting," "sportsmanship," "healthy sports," and so on, words that frequently appeared throughout those pages, and the place in which my poem was printed seemed to form a special zone in isolation from the other contributions, like a kind of foreign settlement. What I had said in the poem or hoped to get across was the symbolic nature of a hunting gun as it had intuitively come to me. I had no need to feel ashamed of the poem. I had even felt something of pride.

If my effort had appeared in another magazine, there wouldn't have been any problem, but this publication belonged to the Hunters Club of Japan, whose aim was to propagandize hunting as a most healthy and manly sport. In such an edition my view of hunting was more or less heretic and should have been rejected. When I fully realized this, I knew how embarrassed my friend must have been when he had read my manuscript, and I appreciated the consideration he had shown me by daring to print it in his magazine, though he must have hesitated before including it. For some time after that I felt guilty about it.

I expected that a member or two of the Hunters Club would send me postcards of protest, but this was because of my own fearful vanity, and long afterwards I hadn't received even one complaint about the poem. Fortunately or unfortunately, it was treated with silent contempt by the hunters of Japan. Or to be more exact, it was probably never read at all.

About two or three months passed, and I had forgotten about it, when I received a letter from one Josuke Misugi, a total stranger.

Centuries back, a historian who commented on the characters engraved on the Taishan monument said they looked like white sunshine after the showers of late autumn have passed. I'm exaggerating somewhat, but the characters on the large envelope of white paper gave a similar impression. We don't know the real beauty and style of the Taishan characters because the stone monument has fallen apart, and not even a rubbed copy is left. Josuke Misugi's huge characters threatened to jump off the envelope. They were robust and gorgeous and flowing, but while I stared at them, I felt a kind of emptiness coming out of each one, and I remembered what the historian had said about the monument. Misugi had soaked his brush in India ink, and probably holding the envelope in his left hand, he seemed to have dashed everything off at one time, but I saw in the writing a queer, cold expressionlessness and an indifference quite unlike the simplicity of maturity. I felt that he didn't pride himself in his skill and that he was without the vanity that usually clings to an expert in calligraphy.

At any rate, the letter was so magnificently and gorgeously written that the crude wooden mailbox of my house seemed inappropriate to hold it. When I opened the envelope, I found he had written on more than six feet of Chinese writing paper, each line containing only five or six huge characters like those on the outside.

18

"I'm somewhat interested in hunting," Misugi wrote, "and recently I had the opportunity of reading your poem. I'm a man without taste, and I haven't any feeling for poetry. To tell the truth, that was the first time I had ever read a poem. Forgive me for telling you that the poem gave me my first opportunity to become acquainted with your name. But I was moved, more than I've ever been, by reading your lines."

The letter began in that way, and when I looked over the words, I felt my heart tighten for a moment as I remembered the poem that had been fading from my own mind. I thought that a protest had come at last—and from no common huntsman. But as I read further, I found that the contents were quite different from what I had expected. Misugi had written of matters I had never dreamed of. Yet his words were always courteous and written in a moderate style with a kind of self-assurance and calm similar to that of his characters.

"What would you say to my telling you that the man you wrote about in your poem is no other person than myself? You probably noticed my rather awkward figure in the village at the foot of the mountain when I went out shooting in the Amagi hunting grounds. My black and white setter, trained especially to go after pheasants, and the Churchill, which my wonderful teacher had given me in London, and even my favorite pipe attracted your attention. All of this certainly overwhelms me. And that my state of mind, which is far from spiritual, inspired you to write a poem makes me feel honored and confused. Now for the first time I greatly admire the uncommonly sharp insight of a poet."

When I had read this far, I tried to recall the huntsman I had come across five months before on my walk along the narrow pass through the cedar trees near, as he said, the small hot-spring village at the bottom of Mount Amagi in Izu. But I couldn't remember anything vividly except the vague impression I had caught of the strangely lonesome back of the hunter. I recalled that he was tall and middle-aged, but the details of his body and features didn't return with any clarity.

Of course I hadn't looked at the man with any particular attention. It was only that the person walking toward me with a gun on his shoulder and a pipe in his mouth had, unlike ordinary hunters, something contemplative about him, and that struck me as peculiarly clean in the cold air of the early winter morning. In spite of myself, I turned back to look at him after we had passed each other. He stepped out of the path he had come along, turned toward the mountain covered with shrub, and started slowly up the fairly sharp slope, carefully shifting his weight with each step as if he were afraid he might slip. As I watched his retreating figure, I got, as I said in my poem, an impression of loneliness. I knew enough to recognize that the dog was a fine setter, but I didn't know the name of the gun since I had never had anything to do with hunting. The night I wrote the poem I learned that a Richard or a Churchill is the finest type of hunting gun in England, and I took the liberty of having him carry the latter on his shoulder. By chance it had turned out to be the one Misugi had carried. For these reasons, even though the hero of the poem was introducing himself in this way, the real Josuke Misugi, the source of my poem, was still unknown to me.

His letter continued: "You may have your doubts

20

about a person who is suddenly bringing up an irrelevant topic. I have here three letters addressed to me. I had intended to burn them, but after reading your excellent poem, I thought I would show them to you. I don't want to disturb your quiet state of mind, yet I'm sending them anyway under separate cover. I would be happy if you would read them at your leisure. I only want you to read them. My wish goes no further than that. I want you to know what the 'white riverbed' is that I have looked into. It seems to me that a man is foolish enough to want another person to understand him. I've never felt this before, but on learning that you were interested in me, I decided to show you everything. After you have read them, I hope you'll burn the three of them for me. You probably noticed me at Izu just after I had received these letters. Several years ago I became interested in hunting, but while at present I am a lonely man with no one around me, all those years I was successfully respectable in both my public and private affairs, and the gun on my shoulder seemed indispensable. Let me just add that much about myself."

Two days later the three letters reached me. They were enclosed in an envelope bearing Josuke Misugi's name and his address, a hotel in Izu, the same as on the former letter to me. Each had been sent to him by a different woman. I read them and—no, at this point I won't put down the impressions I got from them. I'm going to copy the letters here, but before I do, let me add that since Misugi seemed to occupy a fairly high place in society, I searched for his name in *Who's Who* and in some directories and what not but couldn't find it. No doubt he was using a pseudonym. In transcribing these letters, I filled in the name Josuke Misugi in many of the blotted-out portions where originally his true name must have been written. I also used pseudonyms for the other persons in the letters.

SHOKO'S LETTER

Dear Josuke:

Three weeks have passed since mother died, and how the time has rushed by! No more condolence calls have been made since yesterday, and the entire house seems suddenly hushed, and now at last I really feel that mother is no longer in this world. You must be extremely tired. You had the entire management of everything, from sending out notices to relatives to taking care of the midnight meal at the wake. Besides that, since mother's death was unusual, you often talked to the police for me and got through everything with scrupulous care. I can't think of words with which to thank you for all of these favors. And now that you've gone to Tokyo on company business, I'm afraid that you may be worn out after all of these troubles.

But according to the schedule you gave me before leaving, you must have finished your affairs in Tokyo, and by now I suppose you are quite taken with the different kinds of trees at Izu, which, I remember, is bright and clear but somehow suggests a cold, sober picture painted on porcelain. I took up my pen with the hope that you might read this letter during your stay there.

I hoped and tried to write a letter which, after you had read it, would make you want to remain in the pleasant wind with a pipe in your mouth, but I have tried hard and can't. I have failed to get beyond this point in my writing, and I've already wasted a number of sheets of stationery. I hadn't expected any difficulty. I wanted to tell you my feelings without any sophistication, and I wanted to get your approval about something. I've thought and thought about how to say all this, and I have finished, so to speak, the preparations for this letter. But when I pick up my pen, all the things I want to tell you suddenly press in upon me and—no, it's not that way at all. Really, all sorts of sorrows come rushing upon me from every direction, like the white waves at Ashiya on windy days, and these sorrows confuse me. Nevertheless, I'll keep on writing. . . .

Dear Josuke: Shall I confess? I know everything about you and mother. I knew everything the same day mother died. I secretly read mother's diary.

If I had to tell you this directly, how difficult it would be! No matter how hard I might try, it would probably be impossible for me to talk to you coherently. I can only tell you now because this is a letter. It's not that I'm afraid or horrified. I am only sad. Only my tongue is numb with sorrow. Not merely sorrow over you or mother or myself. But over everything—the blue sky above me, the October sunshine, the bark of the crape myrtle, the bamboo leaves in the wind, even the water, stones, and soil—everything visible in nature becomes painted in sad colors when I try to speak. Since the day I read mother's diary, I've known that nature changes its colors two or three times a day—even five or six times—and does so as suddenly as when the sun becomes hidden by clouds. As soon as I think about you and mother, everything around me is different. Did you know that in addition to the more than thirty colors that are usually packed in a paintbox—red, blue, and so on—sorrow has its own color, which is quite visible to human eyes?

I know from the affair between you and mother that there is a love that no one blesses and that no one should bless. Only you and mother know about the love between you—no one else does. Your wife Midori doesn't know about it. I don't know about it. Not one of our relatives knows about it. The neighbors living next to our house and those living across the way and even our dearest friends don't know a thing about it. And they shouldn't. Now that mother has died, only you know about it. And when you leave this world at some future time, not a soul on earth will imagine that once such a love existed. Up to the present time I believed that love was like the sun, bright and glorious, to be blessed forever by God and man. I believed that love grew gradually like a clear stream glittering beautifully in sunshine and making innumerable ripples in the wind and protected by its banks covered with grass, trees, and flowers. I believed that was love. How could I imagine a love unlighted by the sun, flowing from nowhere to nowhere, and buried deep in the earth like an underground stream?

Mother deceived me for thirteen years, and she died deceiving me. No matter what the situation, I couldn't have possibly dreamed we had any secrets. Mother herself always used to say that we were a mother and daughter left alone in this world. The only thing she refused to tell me was why she had divorced my father, but she said I wouldn't be able to understand that until I married. How I wanted to reach that age! It wasn't that I was impatient to know what had gone on between them. It was simply that I knew how hard it was for her to keep things to herself. In fact it seemed intolerable for her. To think that she should have kept another secret from me!

When I was a child, mother told me the story of the wolf that was possessed by a demon and deceived a small rabbit. The wolf was changed into stone because of his sin. Mother deceived me, deceived Midori, deceived everyone. God! what made her do that? What kind of horrible demon got hold of her? Yes, that's what happened. Mother herself used the word "sinner" in her diary: "I and Misugi too will be sinners. And since it is impossible for us not to be sinners, let us be great sinners." Why didn't she use the words "possessed by the devil"? Poor, poor mother—poorer than the wolf that tricked the small rabbit. And yet, that mother and you should have decided to become sinners, great sinners. That love which can't be kept without being sinful must be a sorrowful thing. When I was a child, someone bought me a paperweight at a fair, a red artificial flower in a glass globe. I took it in my hands and walked away, but suddenly I began to cry. No one could have guessed why. Petals frozen immovably in cold glass, petals that couldn't stir, if it was spring or autumn, petals put to death. When I thought how those petals must have felt, I was suddenly filled with sorrow. That same sorrow has returned to me. The love between you and mother was like those petals. . . .

Dear Josuke: Perhaps you're angry that I've secretly read mother's diary. I almost had a premonition the day before her death that she wouldn't recover. Something in her appearance gave me the terrible warning that her last hours were coming. The only thing wrong with her was that she was always slightly feverish these past six months, but she didn't lose her appetite, and as you know, she had a brighter complexion and gained weight. But I couldn't help feeling of late that her back looked ominously forlorn, especially the lines from her neck to her shoulders. The day before she died, Midori came to ask how she was, and I went to mother's room to tell her that she had come, but when I opened the sliding doors I was startled. Mother was sitting on her bed, her face turned away from me, and she was wearing a purple-gray silk *haori* embroidered with large, bright thistles—a coat she had long ago given to me. It was too gay for her, she said, and she had put it away in a chest and had never taken it out until that moment.

"What's wrong?" mother said, turning toward me and wondering what had surprised me.

"Well—" After saying only this, I couldn't think of anything else to add, and a moment later I didn't even know why I had made a face. Instead, I began to laugh. Mother had always been extravagant in her clothing, and it wasn't surprising that she had taken out her bright clothes of earlier years to try them on. Since she had been sick, it had become part of her daily routine to take them out after they had been stored away so long and to put them on, I suppose, to divert herself. But when I think back now, I was nevertheless shocked to find her wearing that silk haori. She looked so beautiful in it that I'm not exaggerating when I say that she seemed dazzling. And yet at the same time she appeared quite lonely. I hadn't noticed that quality about her before. Midori followed me into the room. After her exclamation of "How beautiful!" she sat down for a while without speaking, as if she too were enchanted by its beauty.

During the entire day I remembered that beautiful but terribly lonesome sight of mother's back covered by the haori. It was as though a cold piece of lead had dropped far down in my heart.

Toward evening the wind that had been blowing all day died down, and with the help of our maid Sadayo I raked up the fallen leaves in the garden and burned them. I also decided to get some bundles of rice straw which we had bought at a fantastic price several days before. I thought I would burn them to make a bed of ashes for the charcoal brazier in mother's room. Mother, who had been looking out the window, came out to the veranda with a neat parcel wrapped in colorful paper. "Burn this with them," she said.

"What is it?" I asked.

"Never mind!" she said with unusual sternness. But she probably thought better of it after a while and said calmly: "A diary. It's your mother's diary. Burn the package just as it is." And then turning, she went along the corridor with tottering steps as if the wind were carrying her away.

It took about half an hour to make the ashes. By the time the last piece of rice straw had flared up and turned into purple smoke, I had made up my mind. I secretly got up to my room with the diary and hid it far back on a shelf. That night the wind started again. As I looked down from my upstairs window, I thought that the garden, lit brightly by the terribly white moon, was a bleak and wild beach in some extremely northern country, and the sound of the wind reminded me of breaking waves. Mother and Sadayo had already gone to bed, and I was up alone. After I had piled five or six thick encyclopedia volumes against the door so that it couldn't be opened from outside and had drawn the curtains (I was even afraid of the moonlight flowing into the room), I adjusted the shade of my desk lamp and put the large notebook under the light. . . .

Dear Josuke: I thought that if I missed this chance, I would never know about my father and mother. Until that time I had naively thought of waiting until I could marry to learn about them. But when I had seen mother dressed in that haori, I had changed my mind. It had become my sorrowful secret that she would never get well.

The reasons why they were divorced had leaked out to me from my grandmother at Akashi and from some other relatives. I knew that when I was five years old and living with mother and grandmother and the maids at Akashi, my father was studying for his degree in pediatrics at Kyoto University. One windy day in April, a young woman holding a baby in her arms came to see mother. On entering the guest room, the woman put the baby in the alcove, and to mother's great surprise when she came in bringing tea, she found the woman changing into a nightgown that she had taken out of the basket she was carrying. Of course the woman was insane. We found out later that the ill-fed baby sleeping in the alcove was the child of my father and that woman.

I heard that the baby died soon after that, and the woman, whose insanity was fortunately only of a temporary sort, soon recovered. They say she's now married and living happily with a merchant at Okayama. Shortly after that incident mother left Akashi and took me with her, and my father, who had taken my mother's family name, had to be divorced. When I was old enough to enter a school for girls, grandmother told me: "Saiko was too obstinate. She should have forgiven him."

Was it mother's too great delicacy that wouldn't allow her to pardon my father for his mistake?

That's all I know about them. Until I was seven or eight, I was certain that my father could not possibly be alive. I had been brought up to believe that he was dead. And even now I have that feeling. My father, who's said to be managing a large hospital within an hour from here, my father, who's said to be single even now—that real father, I can't imagine no matter how much I try. If he really is alive, my father—Shoko's father—died a long time ago.

I opened the first page of mother's diary, and the word my devouring eyes first caught sight of was not what I had expected. It was the word sin. Sin, sin, sin. It was there again and again, written so wildly that I couldn't believe I was seeing my mother's handwriting. Under the piled-up "sins," as though she had been suffering under the weight of that word, she had written in disorder only: "God forgive me! Midori-san forgive me!" All the other words disappeared from my view, and only the words from that line seemed to be breathing like ugly demons waiting to pounce on me.

I closed the diary immediately. What a terrible moment that was! Everything was silent around me except the beating of my heart. I got up from my chair to make sure that the doors and windows would not open, and when I came back to my desk, I had enough courage to open the diary again. And feeling as though I myself had changed into a devil, I read it from cover to cover. Not a line had been written about what I was so eager to know, about my parents. I found only the affair between you and mother, an affair I had never dreamed of, written in words so wild that it never occurred to me my mother could use them. Sometimes she suffered, sometimes she was ecstatic, sometimes she prayed, sometimes she was in despair, sometimes she decided to kill herself —yes, she had often thought of committing suicide. She wrote that if by chance Midori should discover what was going on between you and mother, then she would kill herself. To think that mother, who always talked so pleasantly with Midori, should have been so much afraid of her!

After reading the diary, I knew that mother had been burdened with the thought of death during the last thirteen years. Sometimes for four or five days, sometimes for two or three months at a stretch, she didn't make an entry in her diary, but on every page she was facing death: "Death will do. Death settles the entire matter, doesn't it?" Such desperate and meaningless words— what made her write them? "If one is prepared to die, what does a person have to fear? Be more brazen, Saiko!" What made my gentle mother utter such impudent words? Was that love? Was that the beautiful and glorious thing called love? Once on my birthday you gave me a book that had a picture of a proud naked woman by a beautiful spring with her long flowing locks coming down over her breasts, bud-like and upturned and held in her own hands, and the book said that was love. But how different was that love between you two!

From the moment I read mother's diary, Midori changed into the most horrible person in the world. Mother's secret pains have not vanished but have become my own. That Midori who once kissed me with her lips pursed! That Midori I loved so much that it was hard to tell whom I loved more, mother or her! It was no other person than Midori who gave me a knapsack with a picture of a big rose on it to celebrate my entrance into the primary school at Ashiya. When I went to a summer camp, she also gave me a float shaped like a bird. When I was in the second grade, I recited Grimm's "Tom Thumb" on class day and everyone applauded, and it was none other than Midori who helped me rehearse it almost every night and gave me a treat after each rehearsal.

And so on and so on. No matter what I remember of my childhood, I always find your wife there. Midori, my mother's cousin and friend. Midori, who had once been good at mahjong and golf and swimming and skiing, though her only activity now is dancing. Midori, who used to bake a pie bigger than my face. Midori, who surprised mother and me by bringing with her a lot of Takarazuka chorus girls. Why has she always come into our lives with such gaiety as though she were a huge rose?

32

If I ever had any premonition about you and mother, I experienced it only once. And that was about a year ago. I had been walking to school with a friend, and we had come as far as the station when I discovered that I had left my English exercise book at home. I begged my friend to wait for me there, and I went back to get it, but when I got to our front gate, for some reason or other I couldn't go in. Our maid had gone out on an errand that morning, and only mother was supposed to be at home. But her being alone inside made me feel somewhat uneasy. In fact, I was afraid. As I stood in front of the gate and looked at the thick growth of azaleas, I hesitated for a while about whether or not to enter, and finally I gave up the idea of getting the book and went back to my waiting friend. I couldn't explain the strangeness of the feeling. I had the impression that mother's own time had been moving through the house from the moment I had left it to go to school. I felt that if I went in, mother would be embarrassed, and her face would become sad. I walked along kicking the gravel on the road, and when I reached the station, I leaned against the back of the wooden bench in the waiting room without listening to my friend's talk.

This was the first and last time I had that feeling. But this premonition, as I have called it, now seems a horrible one. What a terrible thing that one should have omens! Who can say that Midori has not had the same premonition on some occasion just as I had without any reason? Even while playing cards, Midori, sharper than a pointer, prides herself on getting the scent of the minds of others. It's awful to think about, but my anxiety is certainly ridiculous and unnecessary. Everything's over now.

33

The secret has been kept. No, mother died only to keep the secret. I believe that's why she died.

On that evil day before her pains began, pains that were short but, as one could see, terrible, mother called me and with a strangely calm face like a puppet's in a Bunraku play, said: "I've just taken poison. I'm tired. Tired of living any longer. Tired."

She didn't seem to be talking to me but to God through me, and her voice was strangely clear, like heavenly music. The words sin, sin, sin, which had formed a structure as high as the Eiffel Tower, and everything I had found in her diary the night before—it was all falling down around her. I heard the rumbling sounds quite definitely. The weight of the many-storied buildings of sins which had lasted for thirteen years was now crushing my worn-out mother and carrying her away. I had been sitting on my legs as though I were dazed, and I had been following her glance, which seemed fixed on something in the distance, but I felt an anger coming down on me like a sudden blast at the end of autumn. Whatever it was, it was like anger. A hot, bursting passion of indescribable anger at something—I don't know what. Still watching her face, I said: "I understand."

I said the words as if I had no concern in the matter. But after answering her in that way, I felt my mind become cold and clear as if someone had dashed it with water. And with a strangely calm feeling that surprised even me, I stood up. Instead of going across the guest room, I went down the two long passages like a person walking on water (it was at that time that mother's short cries began, as if she were being engulfed in the black waters of death) and picked up the telephone and called you. But it was Midori, all confused, who rushed into the house five minutes later. Mother died holding the hand of Midori, the person she had loved and feared more than anyone else. Midori put a white cloth over mother's face, and it no longer knew either pain or sorrow. . . .

Dear Josuke: The first night of the wake was so quiet that it's hard to believe such a night was possible. The coming and going of numbers of people, including the police and the doctor and the neighbors—all of that had stopped with the arrival of night, and only you and Midori and I were left before mother's coffin. Each of us was as silent as if we were listening to the sound of water flowing up around us. Every time an incense stick burned to ashes, we would, by taking turns, put in a new one and pray with palms together in front of mother's photograph. Sometimes we opened the window for a change of air. You seemed to be the saddest of us. When you got up to offer a new incense stick, you looked intently and calmly at the photograph, and I seemed to see you smiling faintly in a way no one but my mother could have understood. No matter how difficult mother's life was, she still might have been happy—I thought so many times during the night.

About nine o'clock when I went to the window, I suddenly started to cry. You stood up calmly and put your hand gently on my shoulder for a while and then without saying a word went back to your seat. I didn't cry that time because of my sadness over mother's death. It was because while I was remembering that mother had not even mentioned your name once in her last moments and while I was wondering why Midori had come running instead of you when I telephoned—while I was thinking about such things—I seemed suddenly overwhelmed with sadness. I think it came from pitying you because you and mother had to be actors up until the very end of her life in order to protect your love, and I remembered the petals of the flower crushed in the glass paperweight. Standing up and opening the window and looking at the cold sky full of stars, I suppressed the sorrow that wanted to burst out into a scream, but when I thought that at that moment mother's love was going to heaven through the stars, that her secret love, not known to anyone, was going among the stars, I couldn't resist the impulse to cry out any longer. When I compared the sadness of mother's death with the deep sadness of that love on its way to heaven, her death seemed to me almost insignificant.

When I picked up my chopsticks for the midnight meal, I cried violently once more. Midori said to me in her calm voice and in her gentle way: "Try to control yourself. It's difficult for me not to be able to help you, but I know how you feel."

As I wiped away my tears and looked up at her, I found that she too was in tears. And looking at her beautiful wet eyes, I shook my head silently. She would not have understood that small gesture of mine. To tell the truth, I cried the second time because Midori suddenly seemed pathetic. When I saw her put the food into four small dishes, first to offer to mother, then for you and then for me and last for herself, I somehow suddenly felt that Midori was the one most to be pitied, and that feeling made me burst into a fit of sobbing.

That night I wept once more. I had gone to bed in the next room after you and Midori told me to. You said I would be thoroughly exhausted the next day if I stayed at mother's side all night. When I got into bed, I fell asleep at once, but I soon woke up again, completely drenched with sweat. I glanced at the clock on the side alcove shelf and found that it was only an hour since I had fallen asleep. The room next to mine, in which the coffin had been placed, was as quiet as before, and the only sound I heard was when you occasionally used your lighter. About a half hour passed, and then you said: "Won't you rest for a while, Midori? I'll stay awake."

"No, thank you. Won't you?"

I heard that brief conversation between you and Midori—no more—and everything returned to its former stillness, unbroken after that. Under the covers I cried bitterly for the third time. You would never have heard me then. I wept because everything seemed lonely, sad, and horrible. All three of you—mother, who had already become a soul, and you and Midori—were sitting in a single room, each with secret thoughts and not saying a word about them. When I thought about that, the world of grown-ups seemed unbearably lonely and sad, a horrible world. . . .

Dear Josuke: I have written incoherently about many things, but I tried to express my present state of mind without being untruthful because I want your approval of what I'm going to ask.

It's no more than this: I don't want to see you or Midori any more. I can no longer play the baby to you so artlessly or presume upon Midori's love so innocently,

37

now that I have seen the diary. I want to get out from under the litter of the word "sin" that has crushed mother. I no longer have the spirit to continue writing.

I am leaving the charge of the Ashiya house to Mr. Tsumura, one of my relatives, and I intend to go back to Akashi for the time being and earn my own living by starting a shop, say, in foreign-style dressmaking. Mother advised me in her will to consult you about everything, but if she had seen my present state of mind, she never would have suggested that.

I burned mother's diary in the garden today. The large notebook turned into a handful of ashes, and when I went to get some water to pour over them, a little whirlwind carried everything away together with the dead leaves.

MIDORI'S LETTER

Mr. Josuke Misugi:

When I write your name in this formal way, I feel my heart throbbing with emotion in spite of my age (I'm only thirty-three!) as though I were writing a love letter. I have written scores of such letters during the last ten years, sometimes secretly, sometimes openly, but among all of them not one has been addressed to you. Why? I'm being serious, not flippant, for that realization makes me feel an oddness I can't explain logically. Don't you also think this strange?

Mrs. Takagi (perhaps you know her—I mean the lady that looks like a fox when she puts on make-up) once made character sketches of all the distinguished people living in the wealthy suburbs between Osaka and Kobe. At that time she made a very impolite assertion that as a person you weren't interesting to women, that you couldn't understand the delicate psychology of women, and that if you were ever bewitched by a woman, you wouldn't be able to bewitch her yourself. Of course, that slip of the tongue came while she was slightly drunk, so you shouldn't mind it very much, but all the same, you are like that. First of all, you've never had anything

39

to do with loneliness. You've never felt lonesome. Sometimes you look bored, but your face never really shows wistfulness. No matter what the situation is, your solutions are too clear-cut, and then you believe firmly that your own judgment is always right. You may think you are self-reliant, but somehow it makes one impatient to shake you. In a word, a woman sees you as rather intolerable and finds that you lack the interesting qualities of other men, and she finds it's quite useless to take a fancy to you even if she's inclined to.

So it's probably unreasonable of me to be impatient to make you understand my queer and inexplicable feeling about the fact that among the numbers of letters I've written, not one was addressed to you. And that still seems to me very strange. There could easily have been one or two love letters written to you. Yet, in another way, even though none of them were addressed to you, all the letters I wrote contained my own feelings about you in spite of the fact that different men received them. The explanation seems to be quite simple: since I'm shy by nature, I can't write a sweet letter to my husband. It's as though I remained the naive innocent, so I can't help constantly writing one letter after another to men I can write to with a composed mind. That may be called my evil star, the ill luck I was born with, and at the same time it may be yours.

> Fearful that approach
> May collapse your towering stillness,
> I wonder from afar.

Last autumn while I was thinking of you in your study,

I put down my feelings in this poem. It is a poem about a poor wife's emotions while she kept herself from breaking (I mean she didn't know how to break) the stillness of your study where you might have been examining, say, a white vase of the Yi dynasty. (Ah, how thoroughly guarded, solid, and intolerable a citadel you are!)

You may say I'm lying. But even while playing mahjong all night, I had enough composure of mind to turn my thoughts to you in your study. As you know, the outcome of the poem was, regrettably, to disturb the stillness of a young professor's spirit—I mean that philosophical enthusiast, Mr. Tagami, who has now been promoted from lecturer to assistant professor, so he has fortunately become independent—for I had secretly left the poem on the desk in his apartment. At that time I appeared in the gossip column of a yellow sheet, and I gave you some trouble. I said before that you make one desperate to shake you. Could this event have shaken you even a little?

Well, all of these impudent chatterings will only increase your displeasure. So I'll get on to the main issue.

What do you think? When we look back, our marriage, which exists in name only, seems to have lasted a very long time. Don't you want to end it once and for all? Surely, it's a sad thing to do, but if you've no objections, let's each of us take the proper measures to gain his freedom.

Now that you're going to retire from active participation in various fields (it was quite contrary to what I had expected when I saw your name among those of the businessmen to be purged), I think this is the best chance you have of liquidating our unnatural connection too. I will make my request brief. I would be satisfied to have the villas at Takarazuka and Yase. The Yase residence is of proper size, and the surroundings suit my tastes, so even though I haven't gotten you to agree yet, I've been planning for some time to make it my home and to sell the house at Takarazuka for about two million yen, which I'll live on for the rest of my life. I should say that this is the last of my self-indulgences and the first and last of my extortions, since I've never presumed upon you before.

Though this proposition comes suddenly, don't suppose that for the present I have any elegant boy who can be called my lover. So you don't have to worry that I will be flattered out of the money by anyone. To my regret, I haven't yet found even one man I can call my lover without feeling ashamed. To have a charming and well-groomed nape and a body as fresh and robust as that of an antelope—there are not many men who satisfy those two simple conditions. I admit with regret that at first I was so much fascinated by my husband when I married him that even now, after more than ten years of marriage, I can't escape his attractions.

Speaking of antelopes, I remember reading once in the newspapers that a naked boy was found living among antelopes in the Syrian Desert. What a beautiful picture his was! The coldness of his profile under his disheveled hair, the charm of his legs, which were said to be able to run fifty miles an hour! Even now I can feel my body vibrate when I remember that boy. Intelligent is the word for such a face, and wild, I suppose, the word for such a body.

Now that I have seen that boy's picture, any other man

appears common and extremely dull. If ever unchastity has kindled in your wife's heart, it would have only been that time when I was fascinated by the antelope boy. When I imagine his tight body wet with the night dews of the desert—no, rather, when I think of the clarity of his rare destiny—even now I feel something strange, something wild, going on inside me.

The year before last I became enthusiastic for a while over Matsushiro, a painter of the new school. I shall be very much annoyed if you believe what everyone says about it. At that time your eyes had a queer light of sorrow that certainly resembled pity. But there was nothing to be pitied for. Even so, I was then a little attracted by your eyes. Not so charming as the antelope boy's, but certainly wonderful. When you could have such wonderful eyes, why didn't you look at me like that before? Strength is not the only merit in a man. When your eyes turned to me, they were always the eyes of a man looking at porcelain, weren't they? So I had to be cold and hard and sit still somewhere as if I were a piece of old Kutani china. As a result, I went to Matsushiro's chilly atelier and modeled for him. Setting that matter aside, I at least have a high opinion of his skill in painting a building, though it's rather imitative of Utrillo, and yet there seem to be few painters in present-day Japan who can fix melancholy as a definite feeling (and an extremely fragile feeling) in painting a worthless structure. As for Matsushiro's personality—phew! Below standard! If your mark is one hundred, his is no more than sixty-five. Although he's talented, he's somehow dirty, and although his features are well set, he lacks elegance. When he puts his pipe in his mouth, he does seem rather ridiculous. Perhaps his is the vulgar face of a second-rate painter whose good qualities are all drawn into his work.

In early summer last year I made a pet of Tsumura, the jockey of Blue Honor, the horse that captured the Ministry of Agriculture Prize. At that time your eyes shone maliciously with cold contempt rather than pity. At first, when I passed you in the hall, I thought your eyes reflected the green leaves of the trees outdoors, but afterwards I found I had made a gross mistake. Indeed, I was extremely careless. If I had known what your eyes meant, I might have prepared myself to look at you, either coldly or warmly. At any rate, all of my senses were then benumbed by the beauty of speed, so your medieval way of expressing feelings was quite foreign to me. Yet, just once, I would have liked to show you the clean fighting spirit of Tsumura clinging to the back of that matchless Blue Honor, outstripping more than ten horses one after another in the final stretch. If at that moment you could have seen through the binoculars the figure of that serious and touching creature (of course I mean Tsumura, not Blue Honor), you would no doubt have been infatuated with him yourself.

That boy of twenty-two with a touch of delinquency in him forced himself to better his own record twice simply because I was watching him. This was the first time I had seen such a form of passion. Out of the sheer desire for my praise, he had completely forgotten everything about me while he was on the back of the brown mare, and he changed into a demon of speed. Surely at those times it was the greatest joy of my life to see my love (it was certainly a kind of love) stirred up in an ellipse of 2270 meters because of his water-pure passion.

44

I don't regret a bit having given him those three diamonds I had kept during the war. Yet the jockey's touching quality existed only while he was astride Blue Honor, for once he set his feet on the ground, he was no more than a rude and ignorant boy who couldn't appreciate the flavor of coffee. Of course, I had more of an inducement to be accompanied by that boy with his desperate and reckless fighting spirit trained on horseback than by that writer Senoö or that degenerate Socialist Mitani, but it was no more than that. So finally I arranged a match between the jockey and an eighteen-year-old dancer (also a pet of mine), and I even gave him the money for the wedding.

I've let myself loose in chattering and made a digression. Of course, if I settle at Yase in the north of Kyoto, I will still have too much of a lingering affection for life to retire from it. I have not the slightest intention of living an austere dowager's existence. I will leave to you as a future pastime the business of building a furnace for making porcelain bowls, and I myself will raise flowers. If I sell them to the florists on Shijo Street, they say I will make quite a large profit. With the help of an elderly maid and a young girl and two other women I now have in mind, I can easily raise one or two thousand carnations a year. For the present our house there will be closed to male visitors, for I have really grown sick of rooms that smell of men. Yes, I mean it. Now, for this of all times, I intend to begin anew and to plan my life with a view toward finding my own real happiness.

You may be surprised at this sudden proposal. . . . No, I think you must always have wondered why I didn't make such a proposal before. When I look back to the past, a thousand emotions crowd in to make me wonder how for more than ten years I could have led such a life with you. To a certain extent, I have been labeled a loose woman, and the world must have thought both of us a queer husband and wife, but we have reached this point without incurring any great social disgrace, and sometimes we have even acted in the intimate position of matchmakers. On this point I am worthy of your praise, am I not?

It's very hard to write a farewell letter. I don't like to be maudlin. But I don't like to be too plain either. I would like to make my request for a divorce gracefully and without our hurting one another, but I can't possibly prevent a strange element of affectation from intruding into my letter. After all, a letter of divorce can't be a charming letter, no matter who writes it. If so, I would write a prim and direct letter that would be equal to a letter of divorce. Permit me to write a radically unpleasant letter which will make you even more cold-hearted toward me.

It was February, 1934. About nine o'clock in the morning I was in a room on the second floor of the Atami Hotel, and I remember seeing you in a gray suit on a cliff just below the room. It is the story of an old, old day that's as vague as a dream now. So hear me with a calm heart. How painfully that silk haori with bright thistles struck my eyes! It was worn by a tall and beautiful woman who followed you out. I had not expected that my premonition would be realized so exactly. To learn whether it was groundless or not, I had just arrived, having come all the way by the night train without even taking a nap.

To use a trite phrase, if I had been dreaming, I wanted to snap out of it. I was twenty years old then (the same age as Shoko-san at present). Certainly the shock was too great for a newly married wife who didn't know the ABC's of life. As soon as I had called the boy and paid the bill (making it look all right to him while he was wondering what had happened), I started outside, feeling as if I couldn't sit still in the room any longer. And standing for a while on the pavement in front of the hotel, a hot, burning pain pinioned in my bosom, I hesitated about going toward the sea or up to the station. I started down to the shore, but before I had walked fifty yards, I stopped again. I stood looking at the winter sea, glittering in the sun as if smeared with Prussian blue just squeezed from a tube. After a while I turned my back on the sea, and changing my mind, I made my way to the station. Thinking back now, I realize that that action led me to this time and this place. If I had gone down to the sea where you were, I would have found myself a different person today. But, luckily or unluckily, I didn't. Certainly that was the greatest turning point in my life.

Why didn't I take the path to the sea? The reason is none other than this: I couldn't help feeling that to the beautiful woman five or six years older than I—that is, to cousin Saiko—I was far inferior in every respect: in experience, in knowledge, in talent, in beauty, in tenderness of heart, in the way of holding a coffee cup, in talking about literature, in appreciating music, in putting make-up on my face, in everything. Oh, that humility of mine! The humility of a new wife twenty years old that is expressible only in a pure curve of a painting. Perhaps you've had the experience, when you have jumped into the early autumn sea, of not daring to make a move because, if you did, the coldness of the water would be all the more sharp. In the same way I was afraid to make a move. It was long, long after that I made this bold decision: since you deceived me, I will deceive you too.

You and Saiko-san were once waiting for the express train in the second-class waiting room at Sannomiya Station. Was it a year or so after the Atami Hotel? At that time, standing among the flower-like schoolgirls setting out on an excursion, I hesitated as to whether or not I should go in. Also impressed on my mind is the memory of that night when I stood for a long time before the closed gates of cousin Saiko's house, wondering if I should ring the bell. The insects were chirping loudly, and I kept looking up at the second-floor room where a soft light shone through a small opening in the curtains. I think it was about the same time as that incident at Sannomiya, but was it spring or autumn? As for such memories, I have no sense of season. There were many other episodes that you would groan about if you knew. But after all, I took no definite step. Even that time at the Atami Hotel, I told myself, I hadn't gone down to the sea. Even at that time. . . . And when I recalled that painful sight of the sea glittering Prussian blue, the pain I had scarcely been able to endure before gradually lessened.

There was a period in my life when I was on the verge of madness, but I think time has settled everything between you and me. Like the cooling of a red-hot iron, you became cold-hearted, and I became as cold-hearted as you, and as I became that way, you became all the more so, and in this way we came to make the present cold, fine family—so cold that each of us felt as though his eyelashes were frozen stiff. A cold family? The word "family" is too warm, too human to use here. It would be better, I think you would agree, to call it a citadel. As I remember, for more than ten years, each entrenched in his own citadel, you deceived me and I deceived you (you took the initiative). What a sorrowful transaction a man can make! Our whole life has been built on our secrets from one another. You pretended to take no notice of my many scandalous acts, though sometimes you had a contemptuous, sometimes an unpleasant, sometimes a bored look. I often called out to our maid from the bath to bring me cigarettes. When I came home after having been out, I would take a cinema program from my handbag and fan myself with it. I didn't care whether I was in the guest room or the corridor as I used my French face powder. And after putting down the phone, I would do a waltz step. I invited the stars of the Takarazuka girls' chorus in for a feast, and I posed in the midst of them for a picture. I played mahjong in a padded housecoat. On my birthday I even ordered the maids to put ribbons in their hair, and I invited only students to my riotous party. I knew quite well how those acts of mine would make you frown. But you did not, dared not, even once blame me for my behavior with any severity. So we have never quarreled with each other. And the stillness of the citadel has never been broken. Only, the air hanging there has become strangely rough and wild, irritable to our senses like the heat in the desert. When you could shoot a pheasant or a turtledove with your hunting gun, why couldn't you shoot me through the heart? If you deceived me at all, why didn't you deceive me more cruelly, more thoroughly? A woman can be transfigured into a goddess even by the lies of a man.

But I was able to endure such a life with you for more than ten years, as I remember, only because I had some vague but persistent expectation lurking somewhere in my heart that some day there would be an end to our transaction—something would happen, something would come. Of what that something would be I could expect only two possibilities: either I would lean against you with my eyes closed, or with the penknife you had given me as a souvenir on your return from Egypt, I would stab you in the chest and make you bleed.

Which do you think I hoped for? I myself don't know.

Well, already five years have passed. And there was such an event, do you remember? If I recall correctly, it was just after you had come home from southern Asia. I had been away for two days, and the third day I came home a little tipsy. I thought you had gone to Tokyo on business, and I was surprised to find that you had already returned. You were all alone in the living room, working on your gun. All I said was "Well, here I am," and then I went out to the veranda and sat on the sofa with my back to you, cooling off in the breeze. The awning of the outdoor dining table had been put under the eaves and was propped against one of the glass sliding doors, which reflected part of the living room. I could see your figure there, wiping the barrel of the gun with a white cloth. I had fallen into that languid mood in which one feels worn out with pleasure. I was on edge and yet too tired to move even a finger, and unintentionally I was resting my eyes on your reflection. Having wiped the barrel, you replaced the breechblock, which you had also cleaned. Then you lifted and lowered the gun several times, each time leveling it against your shoulder. But after a while the gun didn't move. It was steadied against your shoulder, and you were aiming with one eye closed. I suddenly stiffened and found the barrel was obviously aimed at my back.

"Is he going to shoot me?" I wondered.

Of course the gun wasn't loaded, but I was interested in seeing if you wanted to kill me. I assumed an unconcerned air and closed my eyes.

"Is he aiming at my shoulder or my back or my neck?"

I waited impatiently for the trigger to click coldly through the quietness of the room. But it never sounded. If I had heard it, I would have fallen down that moment on the spot—I had been preparing to put on such an act as if it had been the cherished aim of my life for many years.

I was losing patience, and I secretly opened my eyes to find you still aiming at me. I sat that way for some time. But suddenly all of it seemed ridiculous, and I made a move. And when I looked at the real view, not the reflection in the window, you swiftly moved the muzzle away from me. You aimed at the Alpine roses which you had transplanted from Mount Amagi and which had bloomed that year for the first time. And at last you pulled the trigger. Why didn't you shoot your unchaste wife? I think I deserved shooting at that time. You had enough intention to murder me, and yet you didn't press the trigger at all. If you had, if you had not put up with my unchastity, if you had shot your hatred through my heart, I might simply and unexpectedly have leaned against you. Or, on the other hand, I might have shown you my own skill in shooting. At any rate, you didn't do it, so I moved my eyes away from the roses that had been substituted for me, and with self-conscious tottering steps and humming a tune, "Sous les toits de Paris" or some such thing, I headed for my room.

After that, many years passed without bringing any such critical moment that might lead to either of those endings. This autumn the flowers of the crape myrtle were the most startling red they had ever been. "Something unusual may happen," I thought. It was a vague premonition, but it was as if I were waiting for that something.

The day before Saiko-san died, I went for the last time to inquire about her health. That day, after more than ten years, I was startled to see again the same haori that had been seared like a nightmare into the retinas of my eyes so long ago in the glaring morning sunshine at Atami. That same haori, with its huge and beautifully distinct purple thistles, was hanging heavily from the fragile shoulders of your worn-out sweetheart. When I came into the room, I cried out: "How beautiful!" and then sat down and tried to calm myself. But when I thought of the reason why she was wearing it under my very nose, I felt the blood rush through me. I knew that all my self-control wouldn't help me. The crime of a woman who had robbed a wife of her husband and the humility of a girl of twenty who had just been married had to be brought together before a court of justice one day. That time seemed to have come. I took out my secret, of which

52

I had never given the slightest hint for more than ten years, and I laid it before the thistle-patterned coat: "Your haori brings back memories, doesn't it?"

With a brief, almost inaudible cry of surprise, she turned toward me. I fixed my eyes exactly on hers and never looked aside. For it was she who should have done so.

"You wore it when you were with my husband at Atami, didn't you? You must excuse me, but I was there that day. I saw everything."

As I expected, the color began to fade from her face while I watched her, and then I saw the muscles around her mouth twitching disgustingly. Really, I felt it was disgusting. She couldn't say a word, and lowering her face, she stared at her white hands on her knees.

At that instant I felt an exhilaration, as if I were under a shower, as if I had been living all those years to achieve that moment. But in another part of my heart, I felt an indescribable sorrow that now one of the two possible ends was definitely approaching. For a long time I sat as I was. I had only to sit there as if glued to the spot. How she must have wished to disappear from my sight!

After a while she was somehow able to raise her pale face, and then she looked intently at me. At that moment I felt she would die. Just then death must have leaped into her. Otherwise she could not have looked so calm. The garden grew dark in the shade and then light in the sun, and the music of the piano next door suddenly stopped.

"No, I don't mind. Now, formally, I give him to you."

I said this and stood up and got the white roses I had brought for her. They had been left on the veranda, and

I put them in the vase on the bookshelf and arranged them a little. And once again I looked down at the narrow nape of her lowered head. And thinking that perhaps this was the last time I would see her (what a horrible premonition!), I said: "Don't worry about it. It all balances out since I've also been deceiving you for more than ten years."

In spite of myself I began to laugh. Her silence, at any rate, was marvelous. During the entire time she had sat there without uttering a word, and with a stillness as if she had been holding her breath. The judgment was done. After that she was free to do as she wished.

Then with self-conscious grace and fine form I quickly left the room.

"Midori-san!"

For the first time I heard her voice behind my back, but without replying, I turned along the passage.

"Oh, you're so pale!"

Aroused by Shoko's voice as she came carrying the tea along the corridor, I suddenly realized that my face had also lost its color.

Now I think you understand quite well why I must divorce you, or rather, why you must divorce me. I am sorry to have written so many rude things, but now our sorrowful transaction of more than ten years seems to have reached a conclusion. I have written all I wish to say. I should be glad to have you write your letter of agreement to our divorce while you are staying at Izu, if possible.

Oh, by the way, I have a rare item of news before I finish. Today, for the first time after many years, instead of the maid's doing it, I cleaned up your study. I thought it a good place for a person to calm himself. It was pleasant sitting on the sofa, and the Ninsei vase, like a burning red flower, was very effective on the bookshelf. I wrote this letter in the study. The Gauguin is not suited to the tone of the room, and besides, I want to bring it with me, if you agree, to the house at Yase. So I took it down without your permission and put up a Vlaminck snow scene instead. Then I arranged your closet and put in your three winter suits and, according to my own taste, I placed a suitable necktie with each. I hope you will also like them.

SAIKO'S LETTER

WHEN YOU read this, I won't be here any longer. I don't know what death is, but I'm certain that my joys, pains, and anxieties will not live on after I'm dead. So many thoughts about you and so many thoughts coming one after another about Shoko will soon disappear from this world. My body, my soul, everything will disappear.

Nevertheless, many hours or many days after I'm gone and have turned into nothing, you will read this letter. And living after me, it will tell you the many thoughts I had while I was alive. As though I were speaking to you, this letter will tell you what I thought and felt—things you don't yet know. And it will be as though you were talking to me and hearing my voice. You will be surprised and sad, and you will scold me. But I know you will never cry. You will only look sad (a look no one but me has ever seen), and you will say: "Don't be foolish, dear." I can clearly see your face and hear your voice.

Therefore, even though I'll be dead, my life will hide itself in this letter until you read it, and the moment you open it and begin to follow from the first word, my life will burn again. And for fifteen or twenty minutes until you read the last word, it will flow into every part of your body and fill your mind with all kinds of thoughts as it did while I was still alive.

What a strange thing a posthumous letter is! Even if it is the life contained in this letter and lasts only fifteen or twenty minutes—yes, if it is only a life that short—I earnestly want to give you my real self. Even though it sounds rather horrible, I now feel that while I was alive I never showed you the real me. The self that is writing this letter is my real self. Yes, only the self that is writing this letter is my self, my real self. . . .

I can still remember the beauty of Mount Tennozan at Yamazaki, its red leaves wet from the showers of late autumn. How could it have revealed such beauty? We sheltered ourselves from the rain under the eaves of the old gate of the famous tea-ceremony house in front of the station and looked up at the mountain rising sharply from the rear of the station and confronting us magnificently, and we held our breath over its beauty. Was that unusual view a capricious trick of the November evening drawing on to darkness? Was it because of the special weather that day, when brief showers came and passed many times in the afternoon? At any rate, the mountain was so colorful and so beautiful that we were rather afraid to climb it. Thirteen years have passed since then, but I still remember quite clearly the beauty of the foliage and the way it brought tears to my eyes.

It was the first time we had been by ourselves. That morning you had taken me all over the suburbs of Kyoto, and by that time I was completely worn out. You must have been tired too. As we climbed the sharp and narrow path of the mountain, you said incoherently: "Love is an obsession. It's all right if I'm obsessed by a teacup. Then why shouldn't I be obsessed by you?" And then you added: "We're the only ones who have seen Tennozan's beauty—seen it by ourselves and at the same time. Now we can never go back."

You sounded like an unmanageable child that frets.

Your insignificant yet desperate words made my resolution collapse as if you had suddenly knocked it down —my resolution to leave you, which I had planned to tell you about that morning. The vague sorrows I felt in your violent words and threats stirred in me the desire of a woman to be loved and crystallized that desire into a flower-like, definite shape.

How easy it was to forgive my own unchastity while I could not possibly forgive my husband's!

You used the word sinner for the first time at the Atami Hotel, and you said: "Let's be sinners." Do you remember?

During the night the wooden shutters of our room facing the sea made rattling sounds in the wind, and when you got up at midnight and opened them to stop the noise, I saw a fishing boat in the offing flare up as if a bonfire were being made. Evidently several lives were on the verge of death, but we felt no horror at all. Only its beauty struck us. But when you closed the shutters, I suddenly grew anxious. And I opened them again at once, but the boat must have burned to the water's edge, and I couldn't see even a spark of fire—only the vast, oily calm on the surface of the black sea.

Until that night I had been trying to leave you. But when I saw the boat burn, I stopped struggling and was willing to obey what seemed like destiny. When you said: "Let's be sinners. Won't you help me deceive Midori as long as we live?" I had no hesitation in replying: "Since we can't help being sinners, let's be great sinners. And as long as we live, we will deceive not only Midori-san but everyone else." And that night for the first time since we had started meeting in secret, I slept soundly.

In the boat that flared up and sank in the sea unnoticed by anyone, I may have seen the end of our helpless love. Even now, as I write this, I have a vision of that boat burning brightly in the darkness. What I saw on the surface of the sea that night was undoubtedly the brief and pathetic torment of a woman consumed by love.

Yet such memories help no one. The thirteen years which began with those events were naturally filled with pain and anguish, but still, I think I have been happier than anyone else. Embraced endearingly in your great affection, I can say that I have been happier than a person hopes to be.

Today, while it was light, I ran over the pages of my diary. I found that I had used the words death, sin, and love too frequently, and they once again reminded me that the way I had followed with you was by no means an easy one. But the weight of that large notebook when I put it on my palm was nevertheless the weight of my happiness.

Sin, sin, sin. I was always haunted with a sense of sin, and I was always facing death. I thought that the moment Midori-san knew about it, I would have to die. If she knew about it, I would pay for my sin with my death. But my happiness was all the more incomparably great.

Who could imagine there was another self different from the self I have written about? (You may think this a conceited and disagreeable way of putting it, but I can't think of any other way to say it.) Yes, in a woman called Saiko, there has been another woman I myself didn't know. Another woman you never knew and never dreamed of.

Once you said that each person has a snake in his body. It was when you had gone to see Dr. Takeda in the Science Department of Kyoto University. While you were talking to him, I waited in the long corridor of that gloomy red brick building and passed the time by looking at one after another of the snakes exhibited in glass cases. When you came out half an hour later, I was somewhat nauseated.

Glancing at the cases, you said by way of a joke: "This is Saiko, this is Midori, and this is me. Everyone's got a snake in him. You don't have to be horrified."

Midori-san's snake was a little sepia-colored one from southern Asia, and the one you said was mine was small, from Australia, completely covered with white dots, its head sharp as a drill. What did you mean by those words? I have never asked you about them, but they struck me as strange, and I could never forget them. I often wondered to myself what each person's snake is, and sometimes I thought it was his egotism, sometimes his jealousy, sometimes his destiny.

Even now I don't know what it is, but certainly just as you said at that time, a snake has been living in me. That snake made its appearance today for the first time. That other self of mine I didn't even know—the one that can't be called by any name other than snake.

60

It appeared this afternoon. When Midori-san came to ask about me and entered my room, I was wearing the purple-gray silk haori that you had long ago ordered from Mito City and that I liked more than any of my other clothing during my youth. Midori-san noticed it when she came in. She seemed to be surprised, for she stopped in the middle of what she had started to say and remained silent for a while. Assuming that she was merely startled at my fantastic choice of a youthful costume, I half-mischievously kept quiet too.

Then looking at me with strangely cold eyes, she said: "This is the haori you wore when you were with Misugi at Atami, isn't it? I saw everything that day."

Her face was surprisingly pale and serious, and her voice was as sharp as if it were a knife she wanted to stab me with.

At that instant I couldn't understand what she had meant by those words. But a moment later, when the importance of what she had said came through to me, I pulled together the neck of my kimono for no apparent reason and automatically sat upright.

"She knows everything. And from so long ago," I thought.

Oddly enough, I felt calm, as if I were standing by the sea in the evening and looking at the tide flowing up toward me from the distance. I almost felt inclined to take her hand and sympathize with her and say: "Ah, you know. You know everything."

The catastrophe I had been so afraid of had now arrived, but I didn't feel the slightest horror. It was as if only the soft sounds of the beach had been filling the space between us. In an instant the veil of the secret that you and I had kept for thirteen years was cruelly torn away, but what I found was quite different from the death I had expected. It was like—how shall I put it?— a sort of calm and peaceful rest. Yes, it was a strange rest. I was extremely relieved. The gloomy and heavy burden that had been hanging on my shoulders was removed, and instead there was only an empty feeling that left me strangely on the verge of tears. I felt I had to think about many things. They did not seem to be things that were dark and sorrowful and horrible, but vast and vacant, calm and restful. I was caught up in a kind of ecstasy that might be called emancipation.

I was sitting absent-mindedly gazing at Midori-san's eyes, yet I wasn't seeing anything. I didn't even hear what she was saying.

When I came to, she was out of the room and walking along the corridor with hurried steps.

"Midori-san!" I called.

Why did I shout out? I myself don't know. I might have wanted her to sit a while longer in front of me. If she had come back, I might have said quite simply without any affectation: "Won't you formally give me your husband?" Or I might have said the opposite, but with the same amount of feeling: "Now the time has come to give your husband back to you."

I don't know which I would have said. In fact, Midori-san didn't come back.

"When Midori-san discovers our secret, I'll die." What a ridiculous thought that was! "Sin, sin, sin." What an empty sense of sin! Must a person who has sold his soul to the devil be a devil himself? Had I been deceiving even God and myself for thirteen years?

Then I slept soundly. When Shoko shook me and I awoke, all my joints ached so painfully that I couldn't even get up. It was as if the fatigue of these last thirteen years had suddenly made itself felt. I found that my uncle was sitting near my pillow. You met him once (he has a contracting business). He had come to ask about my health, but he could stay for only thirty minutes because he was on his way to Osaka on business. He chatted at random for a while, and soon he had to leave. Tying his shoelaces at the entrance, he said: "By the way, Kadota married a while ago."

Kadota—for how many years had I not heard that name? Of course my uncle meant my former husband. He had mentioned the name casually, but it had landed forcefully on my heart.

"When?" My voice trembled so much that I myself was conscious of it.

"Last month or the month before. They say he's built a new home near his hospital at Hyogo."

"Has he?" That was all I could say.

When my uncle left, I walked slowly, step by step, along the corridor, and on my way I leaned against a pillar in the guest room. I suddenly felt faint, as if my body were falling down a ravine. Unintentionally, I put strength into the arm holding the pillar. And when I looked through the window, the trees were trembling in the wind, but they were strangely silent, like the interior of a glass tank in an aquarium.

"Ah, it's all over."

After I had said that, Shoko, who had been standing there without my noticing, said: "What is?"

"I myself don't know."

I heard her laugh, and I felt her hand gently support my back.

"What do you mean? Now you get into bed again."

Urged on by Shoko, I walked back with steady steps, but as I sat down, I felt as though the entire world were caving in all at once. Reclining sideways, propped on one arm, I controlled myself while she was there, though with difficulty. But the moment she went out to the kitchen, I cried terribly, the tears running down my face.

Until that time I had never imagined that the bare fact of Kadota's marriage could shock me so much. What had become of me? After some time—I don't know how long—I could see through the window that Shoko was burning the dead leaves in the garden. The sun had already set. It was the quietest evening I had ever experienced.

"Oh, you've already started the fire," I said in a low voice, feeling as if it had been planned between us for Shoko to purposely make a fire in which to burn my diary.

When I handed my diary to Shoko, I decided to kill myself. I felt the time had come when, no matter what happened, I had to die. It might be better to say that I lost the power to live.

Since leaving me, Kadota had not married again. But only because he had not had the opportunity, for he had gone abroad to study and had been sent to southern Asia during the war. When I look back now, I can see that his remaining single was an invisible yet great support for me as a woman. But even though I use these words, I want you to believe that I have never seen nor wished to see him since our divorce, and only occasionally did I hear fragmentary rumors about him from my relatives at Akashi. As a matter of fact, there had been some years in which I hadn't even recalled his name.

It's night now. After Shoko and the maid had gone to their rooms, I took an album from the bookshelf. Some twenty pictures of Kadota and me were pasted in it.

Several years ago Shoko had said: "Your picture and my father's are pasted in here so that they meet face to face."

I was startled. Of course she had spoken without any deep meaning, but on hearing her words I found that certain pictures we had taken when we were just married happened to be attached on opposite pages, and when the album was shut, our faces came together. At that time I merely said: "Oh, nonsense."

It ended there, but I never forgot her words, and about once a year they would come to mind. I hadn't taken the pictures out or put them in different places until today. Today I felt that it was time to detach them. I have taken Kadota's pictures from my album and put them in Shoko's so that she might keep them a long time as remembrances of her father's younger days.

I didn't know that I had another self. The little snake from Australia that you once said was lurking in me suddenly raised its white-spotted head today. On the other hand, I think the sepia-colored one from southern Asia, Midori-san's, has swallowed our Atami secret with its swift tongue and feigned innocence.

What is the snake each of us is said to have? Egotism,

jealousy, destiny—perhaps it's something like karma that includes all of them, and we can't dispose of it. I'm sorry I will have no more opportunities to ask you about it. Still, the snake in each of us is a sad thing. Once, in a book I was reading, I came across the words "the sorrows of being alive," and as I write this letter, I feel those unassuageable sorrows in my heart. What is this disgusting yet unbearably sad thing that we carry inside us?

Having written this far, I've become aware that I haven't yet written about my real self. The resolutions I had when I took up my pen are apt to collapse, and I seem to be trying to escape from what seems horrible.

The other self I didn't know—what a convenient evasion! I said that today was the first time I was aware of the little snake in my body. I said that it appeared today for the first time.

I lied. It would be false to say so. I must have been aware of its existence long ago.

I feel a terrible pain when I recall the night of August 6, when the district between Osaka and Kobe turned into a sea of fire. Shoko and I had gone into the air-raid shelter that you yourself had built. When the droning sound of the B-29's once more filled the sky over our heads, I suddenly felt an uncontrollable empty loneliness. An inexpressible, depressing loneliness. A blind loneliness. I felt I couldn't sit there any longer, and I went aimlessly out of the shelter. I found you standing there.

From the east to the west the sky was a blurred red. The fire had flared up near your house, but you had come running to me and were standing at the entrance to the shelter. Then I went inside with you, but once there, I began to cry. You and Shoko seemed to think I was hysterical because I was terrified. At that time, or even after, I couldn't have explained my feelings. Forgive me. Embraced in your great affection, greater than I deserved, I was wishing, at the moment you came, that I might go and stand in front of Kadota's shelter by his clean, white-painted hospital at Hyogo. Once I had seen it from a train window. Trembling with that irresistible desire, I was suppressing it with the greatest effort I could manage by crying.

Yet this was not the first time I was aware of the other self in me. Some years before, when you pointed out at Kyoto University that I had a little white snake in me, I felt my feet cramp with horror. I have never been so much afraid of your eyes as at that moment. Perhaps you spoke without any deep meaning, but I felt as though my heart had been probed and my body were shrinking. The sickness brought on by the real snakes was at once driven away by your remark. And when I looked timidly up at your face, you were standing there, somehow absent-minded, looking off into the distance with an unlit cigarette in your mouth. That's quite unusual for you. It might have been my imagination, but I felt that your vacant look was one I had never noticed before. It was only for a moment, and when you turned to me, you wore your usual mild expression.

Until that time I had not firmly grasped that other self of mine, but you had named it, and I came to think of it as a little white snake. As I repeated the phrase many times on the same page of my diary, I imagined the ornament-like figure of a small snake coiling tightly, its spiral becoming smaller toward the top, its head as sharp as a drill and elevated toward heaven. And yet it gave me some comfort to think of my horrible and disgusting self in an image that was clean and somehow suggested the wholehearted and pathetic love of a woman.

"Even God would think this figure of a snake pitiable and pathetic. He would pity it." These were the self-centered thoughts I had. And from that night I seemed to have grown into a greater sinner.

Yes, since I've written this far, I won't hide anything from you. Please don't be angry. During that windy night at Atami, the night when both of us confirmed our pathetic determination to be sinners and to deceive everyone in the world for the sake of keeping our love. . . .

Immediately after vowing that bold love to each other, we had no more to say. I was lying on my back on the well-starched sheet and silently looking up at the darkness overhead. No time has ever been for me so impressively quiet. Was it only a short period? Five or six minutes? Or was it as long as a half-hour or an hour that we remained silently in our separate places?

At that time I felt quite lonely. I was not conscious of you there by my side, and I was hugging my own lonely soul. At that moment we had put up, as it were, a united front to guard our love, but since we were to be as happy as we could possibly be, why had I fallen into such a helpless sadness?

You had made up your mind that night to deceive everyone. I suppose you must have decided not to deceive *me*. But as for me at that time, I meant no exceptions, including even you. "As long as I live, I'll deceive everyone, not only Midori-san and all the world, but you also and even myself. That's the life destined for me." Such a thought had been quietly burning like a will-o'-the-wisp at the bottom of my lonely heart.

I definitely had to break my connection with Kadota. I can't tell whether it was due to affection or hatred. Whatever careless mistake it might have been, I couldn't possibly persuade myself to forgive his unchastity. And for the sake of breaking away from him, I didn't care what became of me or what I would have to do. I had been in real anguish. I had looked with all my strength for something to stifle it. . . .

But how unreasonable! After thirteen years everything seems the same today as it was then.

To love, to be loved—our actions are pathetic. When I was in the second- or third-year class of a girls' school, during an examination on English grammar, we were tested on the active and passive voice of verbs. To strike, to be struck; to see, to be seen. Among many such examples was a brilliant pair: to love, to be loved. As each girl, eagerly looking at the questions and thinking about them, licked the lead of her pencil, someone mischievously started passing around a piece of paper, and the girl behind me gave it to me. When I looked at it, I found a pair of questions: "Do you want to love? Do you want to be loved?" And under the words "want to be loved," many circles had been written in ink or blue or red pencil, while under "want to love" there wasn't a mark. I wasn't in the least an exception, and I added one more small circle under "want to be loved." Even at the age of sixteen or seventeen, when we don't know fully what it is to love or be loved, we women seem to know by instinct already the happiness of being loved.

But during that examination the girl sitting beside me got the scrap of paper, glanced at it, and without hesitation made a big circle with a bold stroke of her pencil in the place where not a mark had been left. She wanted to love. Even now I can remember vividly that at the moment I felt confused, as if someone had suddenly attacked me from behind, though somehow, at the same time, I felt a slight revulsion because of her uncompromising attitude. She was one of the duller students in our class, an inconspicuous and somewhat gloomy girl. I don't know what she has grown up to be—that girl whose hair had a brownish cast and who was always alone. But now, while I am writing this letter, more than twenty years since that time, the face of that lonely girl somehow floats before me as if it were only a short while ago.

When at the end of their lives they lie quietly and turn their faces to the wall of death—the woman who can say she has tasted fully the happiness of being loved and the woman who can say that even though she was unhappy she has loved—to which one would God give the true, quiet rest? Yet, is there anyone on earth who can say before God that she has loved? Yes, there must be. That thin-haired girl may have grown up to be one of those few chosen women. Her hair and clothing may be in disorder, and her body may be scarred, but she can say with pride that she has loved.

How I hate it! I want to get away from it! But I don't know how to get rid of her face, following me again and again no matter how hard I try to drive it away! Why do I have this unbearable anxiety as I face the death that will come in a few hours? I am now getting the deserved punishment of a woman who couldn't stand the pain of loving and who sought the happiness of being loved.

After thirteen years of great happiness because you loved me, I'm sorry to have to write this kind of letter.

The time I thought would definitely come, the time when the boat on fire on the surface of the sea should burn down, that final time has come at last. I am much too tired to live any longer. Now, finally, I think I have shown you the real me. Though it is a life contained in a brief letter and lasts only fifteen or twenty minutes, still it's my real life, Saiko's true life.

Let me say once more at the end of this letter that these thirteen years are as dim as a dream. Yet I have been happy because of your great love. More than anyone else in the world.

WHEN I had finished the letters to Misugi, the night was almost over, but I took out his letter to me from my desk and reread it. While I looked at it, I read again and again those mystifying words at the end: "Several years ago I became interested in hunting, but while at present I am a lonely man with no one around me, all those years I was successfully respectable in both my public and private affairs, and the gun on my shoulder seemed indispensable." I suddenly felt a certain unbearable sadness in his peculiarly standoffish and beautiful handwriting. After Saiko's fashion, I might call that the snake in him.

I got up and went to the northern window of my study and looked at the dark March night where the blue sparks from an electric train were flashing in the distance.

I wondered what those three letters had meant to Misugi and what he had learned from them. But was there anything he could have gained? Hadn't he known quite well both Midori's snake and Saiko's snake before he read them?

I felt the pleasant chilly night air on my face, and I stood there for a long time. A part of my mind seemed to have been drugged. I put my hands on the windowsill, and as if I had been looking at what Misugi called his "white riverbed," I gazed down into the darkness of the narrow, thickly wooded garden just below.